SKANE

A Thriller In Verse

Ben Counter

If there was a goddess she would sing of bloody steel
And of gutter-sullied sunlight in a struggle to reveal
Where the broken hands of hovels try to imitate the sheen
Of the silver-plated circus and the wall to keep it clean
From the ugliness and malice like the waters of the lake
So the only breath of oxygen's the beauty that you make,
And the furtive shoots of greenery grow short among the dead
In the unprotected corners where the concrete cannot spread.

Pass along the avenue with windows full of gold
To the stadium where human stock is shown before it's sold.
Over bridges linking endless streets of homes that look the same
To the luxury and neon to express they won the game.
When you find the corners guarded by robust contracted suits
Who will note down all the number plates and monitor the routes,
You will find a structure much like an aquarium of light
Where among the feast and music all the city's greats alight.

Charitable causes were invoked to gather here
The exalted whom the city was conditioned to revere,
Sitting down to bask together in their glory face to face
While the staff and entertainers rush to cater to their taste
And they demonstrate their virtue when they deign to pay the cost
Of a modicum of cash they wouldn't notice if they lost.
Now the seven dignitaries hadn't come to help the poor
But to thrash out their solution to Proposal 94.
Tear your eyes away from each assembled deity

And refocus your attention on the waiter pouring tea.
A reflection in a window or the pattern of a stain,
Vision sliding off his outline to be filled in by the brain
With an unconsidered static, never registered at all
That's until he spills the gravy or he lets a salver fall.
All the same he is a human, underneath the servant sheen,
Unremembered by the players but the centre of the scene.

Everybody called him Skane, a name conveying nil,
Because he was one of millions surviving on their will,
Just a grey and faceless multitude, an echo of mankind,
Only earning their existence as resources to be mined.
Any one of them could fracture from the pressure out and in,
Be a child that plays with matches, a grenade without a pin,
Be a single drop of poison or a timer running out.
As it happened it was Skane that brutal fortune singled out.

Why he hit that precipice is lost among the din
Of a thousand past atrocities that might apply to him:
Of a loved one suffocating in the trailer of a truck,
An informant disappearing or a loved one to abduct
Or a safety regulation being slyly bribed away
With a warning to the viewers of the clip about to play,
Unsuspecting passers-by whose names are numbered with the dead,
Or a tainted major-domo with a gun against their head.

One of these befell him, only Skane remembers which

Of the bodies locked in concrete, in the trauma ward or fished

From the waters of the harbour or recovered from the wreck,

Was the one that turned his anger into something more direct

To the certainty that no one had the hate to take them on,

That without him time would mark them all as blameless paragons.

So he sent an application to the edifice of glass

And awaited seven oligarchs to sit down at repast.

This Proposal 94 was of concern to all

Of the diners at the table, for it followed from a call

To investigate the finances that were before obscured

In the name of greater power that the scourge of crime be cured.

This impending law was couched in arcane jargon without end

Such that one in fifty citizens were trained to comprehend.

Turned out one among that two percent was kept within the sphere

Of the first among the seven who were therefore gathered here.

Sitting at the table's head, the city's Borgia queen

Just for once without the flock attending on their cash machine,

Like an ancient relic found among the blocks of fallen Rome

Where the clouds of hapless plebians accrued outside her home

In the hope a few denarii might pass from hand to hand

In return for votes and favours, rivals driven from their land.

In the streets of the Subura as it is in present day,

Where the woman known as Legion never failed to get her way.

Legion was her moniker for many were the souls

Who infested her dominion in acquiescent shoals.

Without number were the acolytes who kissed her dress' hem

Duly serving in a task that might besmirch her diadem,

Always ready with a power saw or orthopaedic drill.

Ever legion was the legal team unshackled at her will.

Even greater was the multitude discussing her with dread

As she fertilised the countryside with armies of the dead

"Never waved a hand in benediction quite as clean

As the hand I offer royally, for how could I demean

Its perfection with the faintest spot of wet and vivid red?

For I never held a knife or pulled a trigger," Legion said.

"Never gave a sudden firing to a double-crossing man

With a premature cremation as a funerary plan.

Never blocked a hidden cellar off with mortar trowel and brick

With a certainty the man inside was still among the quick.

"Never got a list of talkers' names and what they said

From a lower-tier informant with a vice around his head.

Barely heard of hurling petrol bombs through every other pane

To ensure a flow of favours under threat of cleansing flame.

Yet the sycophants and weaklings treat me like a common cur

To be rounded up and put to sleep, a faceless amateur,

With a future long and windowless, and staring at the door.

So to bring about this fate they made Proposal 94."

Next around the table, putting crudités away,

With a bearing quite patrician and his temples turning grey,

Every aspect he affected torn directly from the page

Of one holy book or other, was a man of middle age.

What his name was now forgotten, and replaced with something grave,

Of severity sufficient to be echoed 'round the nave.

So the city called him "Gideon", which had a sacred ring,

Sounding grandly theocratic for the church's choir to sing.

Gideon beheld his flock from on his chapel's stage,

Where he ran from tearful piety to incandescent rage,

While they wept and Hallelujah'd, and they tongue-distorting writhed.

This fanatical ensemble were traditionally tithed

For a tenth of all their property, unless they might desire

Revelations of divinity and sacred knowledge higher.

For communion with Gideon the sacrifice was great,

In proportion to the prophecies he would elucidate.

Sessions with the prophet were behind the guarded walls

Of the caverns deep and lightless and the smoky Delphic halls,

Where facsimiles of heaven pulsed against the brutish gate

Of a human comprehension coloured by a dreadful fate

That befell a slave of Satan or a breaker of the trust.

Every supplicant inducted saw their concept turned to dust

Of reality and fiction, of the living and the dead,

So the only truth remaining was what Gideon had said.

Matters temporal alone were governed by the law,

Meaning Gideon was quick to curse Proposal 94.

"Am I not beyond the reach of lawyers' ink or oversight

Of the troglodytes who'll never know the glare of holy light?

Such divinity! A prophet! Sacred! Trusted from on high

With a mission that no human soul could countenance, save I!

To evacuate my chosen flock beyond this dying Earth,

With salvation duly set aside for those who prove their worth."

"Lie some more, you pompous prick," across the table came

Someone's voice that issued from behind a glass of fine champagne.

He was called the Gaoler, master of his concrete diocese,

For to all the city's prisons cells, the Gaoler held the keys.

"From among us all you are the one who pushes faith away.

I would bet a Supermax you don't believe a word you say.

I cannot pretend I stand above the pestilence and rot,

But I never told my brethren I am something I am not."

Master of the cycle made of razor blades and hate,

A Panopticon that ever turns to grind the sinner straight,

A tornado built of crumbling stone that draws us to its maw

To abrade away our reason's skin and leave us bloody raw.

So the Gaoler built this empire on a screaming banner font

That declaims our city's downfall into violence and want

By evoking living symptoms of a criminal disease.

They will wait until it's dark outside for their atrocities.

Every headline called for action cleaning up the streets
Until every ballot handed to the merciful defeats.
"See our leaders watch this crisis escalating out of hand!
So we have to speak the language that the mongrels understand,
With a code that names a minimum for every sin to pay,
And a forge to make a hundred thousand keys to throw away!
Although where to put these miscreants from sentencing so steep?
All I need is public money and I'll build the dungeon deep!"

Tutting like a teacher at the horrors in her care
Was an overpainted woman under mounds of yellow hair
Styled vertical and splendid like a Babel on her head
To invoke a righteous quality in everything she said.
She was known by Sally-Mae, which was her self-anointed brand.
Now she pointed at the Gaoler with a chopstick in her hand.
"This proposal has you laughing with the prisons it will build.
For the rest of us it's curtains if we cannot have it killed."

Is your breathing laboured as an obsolete machine
From inhaling those carcinogens since you were seventeen?
Do you suffer from tumescent growths proliferating wild,
Or a noisome discharge making sure you're sexually reviled?
Intervention-proof addiction or a heaving bellyful
Of malevolent depression, people talking in your skull?
A disorder of digestion like you're swallowing a knife,
Or a thousand more diseases bent on ruining your life?
What would you pay out to see your foul affliction end?

Then find out among the sparkled words of Sally-Mae, your friend.

She explains about the doctors who conspire to keep you ill,

And so manufacture patients who exist for them to bill.

They suppress the boons of nature, but those ancient truths recur

Through the high immortal wisdom now inherited by her

Who, crusading through the medium of paperback and screen,

Helps you banish pharmaceuticals and make your body clean.

Sally-Mae will tell you how the chemo isn't real

And your need for retrovirals is to keep you on the wheel,

How rejecting their placebos is to step upon the road

And the second step is paying up and filling your abode

With devices making isotopes and purifying air,

While anointing and ingesting with the fruits of nature fair.

Let the oils and plant infusions saturate you to the bone,

All available from Sally-Mae for everything you own.

"I've a stack of bullion and paper by the trough

All invested in this medicine that couldn't cure a cough.

Not a licence or a peer-reviewed report among the lot!

This Proposal's aimed at making public everything I've wrought!

They will throw me in a prison and then repossess my stuff,

That's unless you ignoramuses can solve it fast enough."

Since her contribution made to a solution wasn't there,

All that Sally-Mae could offer was a disapproving glare.

"Kill the damned Proposal as it's growing in the womb
So before it is enacted it's already in the tomb!
It's with cowardice the moralising troublemakers act.
When the public turns against them, see how fast they can retract!"
So the Theorist began to speak, a fire in her eyes,
With corrupted creativity engorging her with lies
Which could even take denials and repurpose it as proof.
For the blood with which she brewed them, she'd exsanguinate the truth.

Broadcasts by the Theorist were aimed towards the pack
Who preferred their deaths mysterious and helicopters black,
Who denied responsibility for failings in their life
And accused a shadow government of fabricating strife,
Of experimenting wantonly on true believers' brains
While they spray hallucinations from the holds of aeroplanes.
All adopted by the Theorist and made to interweave
To extract a fevered profit from their craving to believe.

"I proclaimed that shooting of a dozen folks of late
Was achieved by crisis actors on the payroll of the state.
At the same time claiming violence is knowingly provoked
So the people are desensitised when freedom is revoked.
An example of a pair of lies that cannot coexist!
With a brilliance like mine they will believe what I insist.
It's not logic that directs them, but their hollowness within.
Once I realised their weakness, they were always taken in.
"Say this new proposal is a tool for the elite

That the peons blame for empty lives and feeling incomplete.

To deflect the revelation we're the ones who keep them poor,

We concoct a foreign-born cabal who came up with this law

To assist a chosen people to monopolise the wealth.

I can propagate the narrative and watch it pen itself!

All I need is thirty minutes with a microphone online

And you'll hear it echo back to us in twenty-four hours' time."

Then a pursed and scowling mouth was twisted more in speech

From the bearer of the standard for trepanning bore and leech.

Should you find yourself in need of silent partners in a task

Of a medical persuasion, and devoid of questions asked,

Only sounds of leather creaking as it strains against a wrist,

Or the gurgle of a larynx blistered up by toxic mist,

Or inducements whispered to an artificial suicide,

For such extra-legal surgery the Doctor is your guide.

"On the current question, may I hasten to remind

All the company assembled, for the good of humankind

Do I welcome the experiments that others would eschew,

For the law is made by lesser men who fear what we must do

To advance the cause of knowledge of our variable form

And escape the base restrictions with which each of us is born.

So we sacrifice morality to see the world afresh

And illuminate the path to an enlightenment of flesh!

"Think upon the services to medicine I made
By providing for experiments, and of the highest grade,
An array of still-articulated slabs of human meat
For a brand-new pharmaceutical with testing to complete.
For convenience of observation shut inside a box
To be watched by scientific minds outside the orthodox
Who must do their work in darkness obfuscated from the law."
At the Doctor's words the Theorist, elated, took the floor.

"What a lurid web I could create if that became
Comprehended by the public! All those innocents you maim
In an avalanche of horrors, a reflection of their fears!
I can say it was the government and live off it for years."
"Thus my point," replied the Doctor, "Know that come Proposal day,
You have money, you have contacts, who will spirit you away.
If the public knew my business there would be no rap to beat.
They would drag me from theatre and they'd hang me in the street."

Finally, a diner used to quieting his tongue,
With his plate untouched, a hunger keen, and noticeably young.
For the choice of his profession the criterion was rage
And accepting the unlikelihood he would attain an age
Where assessing what he's guilty of would fill him up with shame
And the dulling of his anger would give that emotion rein.
So he lacked an appellation to be pinned on him by time.
All the diners called him 'Vermin', and it suited him just fine.
"Just as well I'm shut out from this charming tete-a-tete

For the single point unanswered is whose blood I have to let.

So establish who's essential for this problem to occur,

And I'll cut them out so clean you'll wonder if they ever were.

I can make it fast as thinking, with no body left behind,

Or they'll know that they are dying if that's what you had in mind.

I can memorise the details so the trail will stop with me.

If a woman is inside the house, I'll take her as my fee."

Even though the diners, for their crimes, were hardly chaste,

Yet among them Vermin conjured up a feeling of distaste.

How his vision always lingered on the curve beneath the clothes,

And to come to his attention was enough to discompose

Any woman with sharp-wittedness enough to recognise

The concoction, lust and hatred, boiling just behind his eyes.

All their flesh he felt was owed him, yet they vetoed every claim.

If those women didn't want him, then those women were to blame.

Presently the hollow excavated in his soul

Rendered Vermin so impervious to bending from the toll

Of the acts of violation that made normal people ill,

He was excellently suited as a tool deployed to kill.

But he still concealed the depths to which the rot had sunken in,

With the manifestos posted like a clarion of sin,

Or the trauma writ in luminol and statements to be read

Then forgotten, for whoever wants such malice in their head?

Vermin left a scar upon the city well before
His employment as a problem-solver knocking at the door
Of whoever threatened trouble for a city's overlord.
In the archives where the lawmen of the city would record
Brutal crimes, some done to women were an evidential void
With a single perpetrator who took pains to see destroyed
Indications of his presence, no description or a name.
He was known by what he said upon the climax of his game.

"Like a flower doling nectar out to hummingbirds
Every woman spreads her petals just enough to get them spurred
Into clamouring to furnish the attention that she craves
At the promise of a drop, while almost all of it she saves
For the blessed few to keep her in the plenty she desires,
To be drained and cast asunder by the supple-bodied liars.
Thus they sow the gulf between the sexes, then they come to reap
The obsession with their filthy bodies, cloven, split and cheap."

Nothing being settled on, the Princes called a halt
To the brewing of the plans for their political assault,
Or campaign of threat, assassination, arson, outright war
And a thousand more solutions to Proposal 94.
They decanted with their retinues towards the western gate
And the parking lot where hangers-on and drivers congregate.
All the Princes save for Vermin, with no toadies of his own,
For his nature of employment ruled he always worked alone.
Rearward of the venue was a scenic balcony

Kept exclusive for a manager or wealthy VIP.

Here the city, from a distance, was a mountain range of light

Or a rising, falling heartbeat wrought in gold and malachite.

But all Vermin saw was rotten teeth inside a broken jaw

As he lit a blessed cigarette and took a hungry draw,

In the absence of a harder drug to calm his angry nerves,

'Til he saw a figure standing in the garb of one who serves.

"Whose conceit is such he will ignore the caveats

That advise on what it means to stand before the King of Rats?

Does it even have a name, this one whose time is overdue,

Who decides his final moments will play out before this view,

For the papers when they mourn another fallen mother's son

With unevidenced assurance he was loved by everyone,

He who thinks he is deserving of a moment in my grace?

If the answer isn't good I'll carve a new one on your face"

Vermin was accustomed to the redolence of fear

In the faces of the populace upon his coming near,

But the waiter did not shudder or befoul all that he wore

And said, "Gossip is, the Preacher has acquired a pretty whore,

A possession guarded jealously and flaunted at the place

Where the preacher tells his flock she proves a heaven-granted grace.

I'm aware you have a hatred for that lying streak of piss,

And would dearly love to take from him an item he would miss."

Vermin never dignified a favour with a word,

Never thanking or acknowledging the treasure he had heard,

Only flicked his cigarette into the uniformer's face.

After spitting on the balcony he exited the place.

And at first he never cared about the rumourmonger's name,

Meaning Skane would go uncredited for Vermin's latest game

To be hunted down and vanquished on a plain of shattered stone

As a trophy made of strangled, cut-off screams and broken bone.

Following the flutter of hosannas in the air,

Past the acolytes in phalanx as a cordon sanitaire,

Was an edifice both brutalist and looming with the weight

Of the ten percent of tithing putting gold upon its gate.

Often Gabriel would take his ministrations on the road,

But returned apace there, bearing new believers as his load,

By the promise of its ticket sales to stand beneath its dome,

Like a force of holy gravity to call the prophet home.

Gabriel, preparing to address the loving herd,

In this temple was attending to perfection of his word

In a chamber rendered lavishly in silver gilt and red

With his apotheosis painted on the ceiling overhead.

In the corner was a woman with her eyes still pink and wet.

When he spoke to her it sounded like an owner with his pet.

"Now, you know I like to come here in the evening to rehearse.

Why do you insist on hiding when you'll only make it worse?"

"Carping that I left your pretty face in disrepair

When compelled to acts that hurt you by excessive heights of care,

Is especially galling given how you know full well

Disobedience you show me gets me furious as hell.

Yet invisible I find you when your duty comes around,

And as slippery as mercury, yet golden you are crowned

As a gift bestowed upon our flock by my divinity.

All you have to do is radiate your gorgeousness on me."

"Even now you shirk the obligation to the church

To be beauty made incarnate, but continue to besmirch

The perfected mask I gave you with the ugliness of tears,

Although if you knuckled down to me you'd circumvent your fears.

It's the wilful state of misery that drives your waywardness

And demands that I control you to make something of this mess.

So for God's sake, woman, clean yourself, and dress up nicer too.

And be grateful that for everything, I have forgiven you."

Flinging at her silken clothes he wanted her to wear,

To the vaulted auditorium with praises in the air

For his sermon Gideon repaired, demanding they atone,

Leaving Berenice enrobing in the darkness and alone.

Very rarely Gideon would stoop to call her by this name

Even though he chose it, setting her identity aflame.

Long ago a man had married her, but Preacher had his way

When he put him in a barrel and he threw it in the bay.

Berenice was changing when the shade of shadow changed
To a colder tone that told her how her fate was re-arranged.
Even though her lot was bad enough, a feeling made her sure
That a more accursed future made the minutes next obscure.
As a crowning of her thinking, like a kraken from the sea,
Rose a silhouette, misshapen, bent and brandishing a key.
As the congregation's voices met the swelling organ's boom
It was Vermin stalking silent into Berenice's room.

"Word around the water cooler said there was a bird
In a marble-coated sacristy, belittled and unheard,
So her master would go ignorant his birdie's being plucked
And would never give the order for his pet to self-destruct.
Only after giving sermons would he come to realise
His belongings had been plundered while he sought to canonise
Every single word he uttered for the faithful flock of his.
So I found the birdie's cage and can establish: here she is!

"Not that you will know it but the minutes I foresee
To immediately follow have a certain lack of me
Being subject to a vengeance for the outrages to come
Perpetrated on your body, meaning down among the scum
Will I seek again the contact who informed me of your grace
In the grave misapprehension he would buy himself a place
Running with the Prince of Vermin as his payment for this slut,
But I lifted his I.D. and he's a witness to be cut."
Vermin's face told Berenice she was about to die

So she drew a needle from a brooch to stick it in his eye.

As her sinews bunched to pierce him with that fragile point of steel,

The disrobing chamber doors were thundered open to the peal

Of the congregation's praise reverberating through the hall,

And the prophet of the faithful stood protected by the wall

Of a black-besuited phalanx of the Preacher's recent hires,

All with toecaps in their polished shoes and necks like tractor tires.

"Foolish is the pagan who assumes a blinded eye

On the part of he who witnesses a vision from on high

Of a poison-spitting viper in the bosom of his shrine,

With its purpose violation of a trinket that is mine.

Did you truly have a notion you could take a thing of worth

From the presence of the demiurge's messenger on Earth?"

It was thus the Prophet ordered Vermin taken to his doom,

From the sightline of the camera in the corner of the room.

Dragging by the collar at the summit of his lust,

To the barrel-vaulted nave the Prophet's heavies Vermin thrust,

Where a velvet-covered altar stood before a heaving crowd

Of evangelised fanatics all hosanna-ing aloud

At the sight of Vermin, clear to them an image of the damned,

And of Gideon above him with a dagger in his hand.

With a holy sigh the Prophet gave the silver blade a kiss.

"Dearest brothers, sisters, we all knew that it would come to this.

"Was there ever any doubting in a corner of your brain
That your saviour's ascension could occur if we abstain
From the cleansing of this ground and consecration made afresh
That can only be afforded by the rending of the flesh?
Not a word of horror whispered, or expression of surprise,
Or the flinching of an eyelid will I suffer to arise
At the anti-revelation, for a true believer knows
That the journey's only finished when the claret fairly flows!

"By the thunder breaking from the storming in my soul
And the shining angels lighting up the path towards my goal,
By the thousand names divinity has branded on my flesh
And the powers who have chosen me to make the world afresh,
By the faces of the Maker that in me have taken form,
In their name I make this sacrifice, my honour to perform!
For no longer can our prayers reach the heavens from the mud,
So devotion's signifier must be written out in blood!"

Gideon now held the dagger, bright with candleglow,
So to send his victim screaming to a fiery lake below,
When the Prince of Rats beheld the silver dagger with a smirk,
As if painful mutilation would not be its handiwork.
As the congregation waited for this man's apocalypse
They perceived a mocking chuckle on the sacrifice's lips.
As his last pronouncement, smiling at the Prophet, Vermin said,
"If you bastards think you hate me now, just wait until I'm dead."
Long would those assembled speak of when the dagger fell

Right through sternum, lung and diaphragm, and long would they retell
How he dragged it through the abdomen, upwelling waves of gore,
Parting muscle, skin and organ to the faith-affirming roar
Of believers with a trauma deep enough to culminate
In a need to feel belonging that their Prophet turned to hate.
And when Gabriel withdrew it and the altar cloth was soaked,
There had never been adherents to their leader closer yoked.

Vermin's flesh was barely rent, the deed was barely done,
When the word had crossed the city like the bullet from a gun,
Like the stain from Vermin's body turning holy white to red,
Was the burning revelation that the Prince of Rats was dead.
In the butcher shops and alleyways, the places in the dark,
In the shelters where the victims tried to scrape away his mark,
From the gutters to the helipads the whisper took the news,
And applied a lick of flame to Vermin's long-secreted fuse.

Think again of princes as they took a seat to dine
And to parcel out the city over finger food and wine,
Where one even unacquainted would perceive among them one
Looked upon with naked hate and spoken of by everyone
As an evil to be countenanced, and barely even so,
For his use, that of an animal, just point and let him go,
As a hateful guided weapon, as a dog with fever keen,
To be set upon the business that the princes thought unclean.

Vermin knew for certain, from the moment he could think,

He would die a youth, and bloodily, assaulted in the clink,

Or impaled by quick stiletto blades a moment from the reach

Of a streetlamp, or the target of a bullet sent to teach

What occurs to human refuse when they dare to raise the ire

Of the sort who will express themselves with chains of leaden fire.

But more likely, Vermin knew, his cancellation would descend

From the Princes of the city when his use was at an end.

Knowing no one loved him well enough to mourn his fall,

Even less enough to seek revenge, so Vermin took it all

On his shoulders, full of hatred for betrayals yet to come,

To exact a brutal punishment against whichever one

Of the Princes was responsible for severing the thread

That alone suspended him above the kingdom of the dead.

When the Prophet was confirmed as Vermin's executing hand,

That's when Gideon's became the downfall Vermin had foreplanned.

From a vault where, long ago, the keepers Vermin bribed,

Was retrieved a cache of papers with the Prophet's name inscribed,

With a dossier of data Vermin gathered on the Prince

Of his dealings as a charlatan and every swindle since,

All the tithings and indulgences of Gideon's devise

All connected by a labyrinth of numbers, names and lies.

Not a physical, but information treasure for his use,

That without a hint of irony he'd called the Golden Goose.

Vermin's last instruction to the wardens of the vault

Was to use the Golden Goose as informational assault
By disseminating, once the mass of data was unsealed,
All the info to the Princes, with its provenance concealed.
For within the web of money was a hidden venom thorn
Just as lethal as a dagger, inescapable as morn.
It was proof the Golden Goose was built around a stolen core
That once Gideon had stolen from the Legion long before.

Came the hour that Legion held an audience of crows,
Of the cuckoo-birds and vultures that attended her in throes
And in in fevered fits of wanting, needed patronage again
In return for nameless favours to be called upon just when
Their achievements rode a summit where their usefulness was fit
To be harvested by Legion, who despatched a holy writ
That a body be dismembered or a signature obtained.
But as soon as Legion read the news, she bilious exclaimed,

"Get your filthy hides from underneath my portico,
And decant your glasses back into my bottles when you go!
Just be grateful I do not command you must regurgitate
All the fruits of honest labour that you sycophants just ate!"
Knowing well the consequences that a would-be suicide
Would encounter if the Legion's word was knowingly defied,
The assembled buttock-kissers quit their benefactor's stage,
Leaving Legion on the doorstep, isolated in her rage.

Legion had been given, by her major-domo's hand,

The description of the Prophet feathering his holy land

With the riches he embezzled from a corporation shell,

One created for the laundering of Legion's wishing well

And its stream of filthy money used to buy the patron's grace,

So the loss it represented was a slap in Legion's face.

"What egregious imbecility to take a cent from me!"

Spluttered Legion to her adjutant, "What vital agony!"

"Bring to me a man with an embarrassment of skills

For performing never-traceable, unarguable kills.

Not a butcher knowing nothing of the protocols of death,

But a murderer who honours the cessation of the breath.

Let it not be said upon my word another prince has died!

For the Prophet chose this long ago, the moment he defied

The authority I clawed with bloody fingers from the clay.

It was Gideon who purchased death. It comes for him today."

Legion's major-domo was obedient and tame.

She considered him her property and never learned his name.

"At the station in the shadow his cathedral casts around,

Is a sergeant on the payroll whom our operation found

Discontented and beholden to our cancelling his debts,

Who anticipates your summons every message that he gets.

What is more, he serves their weapons unit. Recently, I hear,

The award with merits high was given, Marksman of the Year."

Legion ordered, "Give this sergeant everything he asks,

And a means of disappearance on completion of his tasks.

Better keep his name away from me, and doubly his face,

But arrange a car and weapon sterilised of every trace

Of a hand to be untainted by the stink of bullet lead."

"As you say, so I shall execute," the major-domo said.

With a weariness apparent, Legion poured a shot of gin

And she took a seat to wait for news of death to trickle in.

Cops who served the district where the great cathedral stood

Were crusaders seeking justice in a bloodied brotherhood,

That were barely ever implicated should dispute arise

Over inconsistent stories when a key informant dies,

Or when substances illicit made to vanish from the place

Where the evidence was kept to be presented in a case.

The elite of this constabulary, envied, every one,

Was the Weapons Unit, blessed knightly order of the gun.

Changing in the locker-room, his minutes counting down,

Was a rifle-toting paladin of notable renown.

He was Officer DiMarco, and the rushing of his thoughts

Were of training in the killing-house and .308 reports.

With the trilling of his phone the interruption broke the train,

So DiMarco checked the message, and the freezing of his veins

Came about because the compromises deep within his past

Were now coming due, the sword of Damocles would fall at last.

No one asked DiMarco of the time the Weapons Team
Were attending to a hostage situation, and would deem
The offender was a danger undeserving of their grace,
For the gun that he had smuggled in was pointing at the face
Of a neighbour who resided in the same apartment tower.
He demanded new employment, restoration of his power,
A confession from the city they had covered up the proof
Of the gunman's noble title, and a chopper on the roof.

At the note of desperation in the hostage-taker's voice,
The negotiator hung up. If there ever was a choice
It had passed an hour before. But on the overlooking heights
Was DiMarco on his belly with the psycho in his sights.
So he disengaged the safety, blinked away a bead of sweat,
And he put a single round into the villain's silhouette.
Through the heart and lungs the bullet carved a bloody avenue,
And DiMarco took his trophy with a perfect through-and-through.

Bullets have a thirst beyond the first initial kill
And are rarely known for stopping when we'd rather they were still.
So DiMarco's shot would exit through the perpetrator's spine
And continue through the wall to where, oblivious, supine,
Wholly innocent, asleep and in her bedroom lay alone
The adjacent neighbour's daughter, with her presence there unknown
To DiMarco when he took the shot, for no-one sought to check,
Though the bullet found her quickly when it thudded through her neck.
It was when the city brought DiMarco up in court

To be butchered as a sacrifice to help the public thought
In the favour of authority that claims to mean them well,
That the prisoner received a guest to join him in his cell.
"What affront it is to see injustice done to such as you!"
Lectured Legion with her lawyer by her side, "And I construe
These proceedings as assault upon the city, to me dear,
But afeared let us not be, my man, deliverance is here!"

Legion sent a legal team with oratory skill
That would make the angels all agree to follow Herod's will.
So DiMarco walked to freedom when the city's charge dissolved,
And he never had a doubt this fortune's payment was foretold,
An opinion the message now confirmed, and so he changed
Into nondescript apparel, and he called in at the range
For a practice with a rifle with a rotor-action bolt
And a calibre to put a tunnel through a banking vault.

Then a car from evidence, impounded moving dope,
And binoculars, a biped and a variable scope
Were collected for the mission, but he only took a pair
Of the fully-powered cartridges, for targets that are there
When the first attempt has missed and the gun's report is heard
And have loitered for the second, never loiter for the third.
With the arsenal assembled and a squealing of the tyres,
He departed for the skyline broken through by holy spires.

Parking at the threshold of the Prophet's sacred home,

The assassin saw a woman in an alleyway alone.

When DiMarco disembarked, she saw the rifle in his arms

And remarked "Though I don't know you, if you wish to do some harm

To the master of the golden-hued cathedral over there,

You'll be piled upon by zealots long before you get to where

You can draw a line of sight across the incense-heavy nave.

But another way remains to put the Prophet in the grave.

"Gideon had built up in the rafters, tucked away,

So positioned that the breaking of the summer solstice day

Would appear to bathe his lectern in a shaft of blessed light,

An emblazoned circle window overlooking from a height.

It is rendered near-invisible, except when looking down

From the rooftop of an office block a half a mile uptown.

Of course, I just told you nothing. Should the Prophet turn up dead,

I was never even here." "Why, thank you ma'am," DiMarco said.

As the rifle-toting stranger calmly pulled away,

Now a second man approached the woman in the alleyway.

He was dressed up in a uniform with braces and a tie,

And a badge that named him 'Skane'. He told her gently, "Madame, I

Understand your name is Berenice, and recently have fled

From the circle of the Prophet, with no place to rest your head.

I would be devoid of pity if I left you here alone.

I can offer you a couch to sleep on, if I take you home."

Berenice regarded this unprepossessing guy

With a face that burdened no-one's recollection, standing by

An unsafe-appearing moped, second helmet on the back,

And declared "The way you know my name is knowledge I can lack,

But to yet another man I am a treasure to be saved,

Or a prize demurely waiting past the dangers to be braved,

And then exhibited in public, your admirers to enthral,

Or amuse you with the prettiness I seem to owe you all.

"Never will I walk again through diamond-spattered gates

To a house a man inhabits, and where everything he hates

Is embodied in a woman so revenge is manifest

By controlling her and thus defanging concepts he detests.

His frustration and inadequacy given form in me,

As a dominated trophy to be shown in company.

I would sooner haunt the bloody streets than wear the golden chains!

That's assuming you're no predator with killing in his veins.

"Nothing is to say you will not butcher me alive

And conceal my sundered body in the city trash when I've

Been denuded of my flesh. Or I'm a project you can steer,

Fit this female to the mould of how a woman should appear.

Quite impossible for any but a smart and moral man,

To defeat my woman's failing in accordance with his plan!

I will brave the city searching for the life unchained I dreamed.

Rather that than bauble, victim, or the gods forbid, redeemed."

Berenice had walked away to vanish in the night

As DiMarco hit the stairs to reach the rooftop at the height

Where the elevated window of the great cathedral gazed

On the face of Prophet Gideon as, hands and eyes upraised,

He proclaimed the holy bounty guaranteed to fall as rain

From the heavens on the faithful in an echo of the pain

Undergone by Vermin on the sodden altar as he bled.

And DiMarco had his crosshairs hover on the Prophet's head.

Soaring voice that echoed from the Prophet's sainted throat,

With vibrato like a pulsing star to fuel the strident note!

First a song he sang to praise himself, his spirit to exhort,

Then a crack from half a mile away that cut the prayer short.

At the altar Vermin's blood had soaked now stood, in mid-reprise,

Holy Gideon, a trickle vivid red between his eyes.

When the silence fell, the Prophet stood dumbfounded in the lull.

And the altarpiece was painted with the contents of his skull.

Barely had the body hit the brain-besodden ground

Than the news of Gideon's demise was orbiting around,

From the gutters to the pinnacles, and settling upon

The attention of those prospering from learning he was gone.

When the Gaoler heard, his lobbying of unelected tsars

To amend the law and put a generation under bars,

Was distracted by his learning that his fellow Prince was dead

When a yet-unnamed assassin put a bullet in his head.

Legion, with a certain savage satisfaction, learned

Of the killing from the master bedroom's radio and turned

To a lover, temporary cure for boredom, to declare,

"That one always said I'd go to hell, looks like he beat me there."

While the Theorist, in makeup for her show, let out a cry

So alarming that the artist got the blusher in her eye.

But the Doctor barely flinched to know the Prophet's lack of life,

For emotions he excised as if he did it with a knife.

Sally-Mae had not the time to think upon the news,

For it reached her in the pastel-coloured anteroom she used

For appointments with the desperate who paid a decade's wage

In a consultation guaranteed to see them to an age

Far beyond the meagre scope that was on offer from the lies

Of the hospital accountants and the system that relies

On encouraging the sickness to destroy them from within.

Or so Sally-Mae would tell them as the nurses wheeled them in.

Tragic was the case that Sally-Mae that day had heard,

Of aggressive cancer, but the pseudo-doctor, undeterred,

Took the patient's hand and with a caring tilting of the head,

Gave pronouncement of a panacea, anciently unsaid

To miraculously banish every ailment of the blood,

With its name, by medical conspirators, drawn through the mud.

But now Sally-Mae would triumph where the doctors got it wrong

And prescribed to last a lifetime, for she knew that wasn't long.

Meanwhile in her studio, and bent over the sink,

As she washed her stinging eye, the Theorist began to think,

As the other Princes surely were, that recently cut loose

Was the motherlode of riches that they called the Golden Goose.

Now uncoupled from the fortunes of the Prophet, it was free

To be plundered by survivors of the evening's revelry.

And while anything but equal splitting should be most uncouth,

Well aware she was, the Theorist, it wouldn't be the truth.

"Every Prince exceeds me in their power," she opined,

Though to no one in particular, "and I am of a mind

To ensure the Golden Goose will not be used to widen more

The divide between myself and every fellow carnivore

Who will carve a bigger portion of the Prophet's mighty work,

Then dismember me as if I were a carcass in the murk

And they hungered for the carrion decaying on my bones.

After feasting they would see one less to challenge for their thrones.

"Silently I will not shuffle to obscurity,

Or be suicided, followed by a florid eulogy

With a subtle message woven to remind, among the grace,

What befalls a Prince who falters in the art of keeping pace.

I may never match my fellows in resources, strength of arm,

Or the ill-begotten dealings with the aim of doing harm,

But no equal have I growing thoughts within a willing head.

If I cannot have the Goose, I will devalue it instead."

Energised, the Theorist convened her loyal clan

Of producers she berated into cooking up a plan

To propel into the public sunlight, scorching in the glare,

Revelations of the Prophet's irreligious wealth, and where

Every penny would be headed through a labyrinth of wire,

To a cataract of money for the Princes to admire.

As the Theorist's producers scattered quick about their task,

There was one who served their mistress underneath a traitor's mask.

At a close facility the Gaoler had in store,

Kept maintained awaiting retroactive changes to the law,

An electric steed of timber, rivets, leather straps and wire

With a crown of steel electrodes fit to set a brain on fire.

It was blackened with the patina of fifty human hides.

On its seat were branded images of fifty men's backsides.

On the arms were furrows dug by fingers clenching from the shock

Of the culminating scene: the play had opened in the dock.

Going by the plan to which the Theorist adhered,

With alacrity the Gaoler, as the time of broadcast neared,

Sent a flunky to the chamber where the execution stench

Festered heavy in the air, to locate the chair and wrench

From its mountings on the floor this looming punisher of sin,

And transport it to the studio before she could begin

The exposé of the Golden Goose, and though he cut it fine,

The electric chair was ushered in beneath the On Air sign.

Monument to death it may have been, but at a glance
It resembled, in a studio unlit and seen askance,
A component of the set, with colours bold and hint of chrome
To imply authority to bring the truth to every home.
So the Theorist, with script compiled to basest fears appealed,
To describe the Golden Goose and all the riches it concealed,
All oblivious she took her seat, no danger any saw,
As her buttocks settled where a hundred dead ones had before.

Credits rolling opened up a deluge from her soul,
Exclamation points of history deleted from the roll
Of atrocities, while new abominations took a face
From descriptions that the Theorist delivered, at a pace
Understandable to only zealots wedded to her lie,
Of coincidence concealing malediction from on high,
Orchestrated by the latest demographic that provoked
From her acolytes a hatred fairly begging to be stoked.

Watching from behind a camera, blinking out a bead
Of anxiety-engendered sweat, tormented by her screed,
A producer let the Theorist attain a frenzied state
Too oblivious to all around to differentiate
A devoted loyal servant from a sabotaging foe
Masquerading with intention to betray with all they know
To a master bent on doing to the Theorist some harm.
Such a traitor watched her, fighting with the strain of staying calm.
Tumbling from the Theorist, a seething, rancid, hot

And climactic high crescendo of her oft-disproven rot

Was erupting past the traitor, who had changed his parking space

When that afternoon he realised he'd have to leave the place

In a hurry through the chaos when betrayal's will was done.

Now uncomprehending how the many parts, him being one,

Were to mesh, and as the ranting reached the signal level which

Was to be his cue, he let his finger fall upon the switch.

Many is the soul who in the year to come would lose,

To a short and viral video with half a billion views,

Frequent hours of sleep from trauma after witnessing the sight

Of a woman in the midst of a polemic, gripping tight

To the armrests of a chair of blackened oak and rusted steel

While the camera held her tightly, framing perfect to reveal

As with rolling eyes she shuddered, with the strain her jacket tore,

And the muscles were like cables standing out below her jaw.

Devotees of theories on government and race

Were repulsed to see the humours of her eyes run down her face,

As emitting sparks between her teeth before they clamped to snip

Through a tongue that stirred a liar's cauldron, severing the tip,

The emitter of a cognitive effluvium now turned

To exude a pall of smoke, acrid and choking, as she burned.

The aroma waxed intensity with every volt and watt,

Like an over-cooked abundance of a fare begun to rot.

Coiling thick, a stinging fog suffused with an array,
A kaleidoscope of odours in mosaical bouquet.
Incandescent steel and cable from the execution seat,
With erupting blood in undertone and notes of turning meat.
Still convulsing, her contorted frame continued to pollute
Its surroundings with the melting polyester of her suit.
At a thousand screens the viewers saw her broken members thresh
As her skin began to bubble, deflagrating from her flesh.

This occasion gave no Prince a need to ferret out
Information on the Gaoler's plot, for everywhere about
Was the clamour of sensation that the Theorist had made
Quite the spectacle of her demise, and not by much delayed
Were the tales of how a prince had channelled voltage to exceed
Her capacity to live before her people cut the feed.
Thusly Sally-Mae would hear a patient chatter from their bed,
While absorbing patent medicines, the Theorist was dead.

Quackery monopolised her working day, and yet
Her imagination pictured how a future path was set
With the Golden Goose apportioned with a quarter gone to each
Of the Princes yet surviving. But not the threat of breach
In the compact made between them caused to Sally-Mae a fear,
Nor the fact the money's total was denied to her. Severe
Was the apprehension striking that indulging in the hoard
Of the Prophet's golden motherlode was someone she abhorred.
Sally-Mae considered this while in the office where,

In a pastel-cushioned womb of honeysuckle-scented air
Overlooked by framed certificates that genuinely meant
She possessed a passing knowledge of the body's fundament,
And appreciated fully the concoctions she prescribed
Were but water with a pinch of salt and colouring, she cried,
"Not enough I must be satisfied with fractions of the wealth,
An arrangement manifestly not conducive to my health!

"I recall the feeling of my skin attempting flight
From my skeleton upon the loathing catching soul alight,
When I learned the presence must be borne, the very air be shared
With a man so porcine, gross and charismatically impaired
That the stench of cancer suffers' disintegrating bowel
From the lack of working medicine, would strike me not as foul
As to look upon that mass of sweat and arrogance I hate.
Now the Princes number fewer, so his blight will concentrate!

"Rather jolly creditors flamenco on my face
As they suckle on my bank account and repossess my place,
Or I crawl unclothed, debasing through the city's grander park,
As a mob observes my penance and my roots go heathen dark,
Than I suffer even momentary knowledge that a suit
Stuffed with crapulence and smugness is partaking of the fruit
Of the Princes' labours. How my very comprehensions strive
To escape the rancid certainty the Gaoler is alive!

"Whether my revulsion bubbles up from such a place
Separated from emotion by enlightened logic's grace,
Or is born of mindless hatred with unnecessary grit
Disproportionate to any act the Gaoler might commit,
And has no compelling reason, is irrelevant to me.
For a time when raising blades against the Princes fatally
Was prohibited by common acclimation died as soon
As the bullet sprayed the Prophet's cerebellum 'cross the room.

"Open season just began on hunting down my peers,
So an ancient pact unwritten is the least among my fears
In comparison to slipping through the surface of the lake
As irrelevance consumes me while the other Princes make
An abundance from the city's flesh. I stutter not at all
to demand I hold the Gaoler's head." She left to make a call,
And discovered how, within the hour, the Gaoler would prevail
On a gaggle of investors at a meeting in his jail.

Progress in these happenings had meaning not at all
To the minions in a building made offensive by the pall
Of the Theorist, whose underlings were happy to ignore
The transpirings while they sponged her sooty fat from the décor.
In a changing room was Skane, who there put on a charcoal suit,
Since the colour was appropriate, and mirrored the repute
Of a studio executive, for, padding his CV,
He'd acquired a second job among the channel's coterie.
Skane entered a meeting room to fall in with a set

Of executives debating, marinating in their sweat,

The solution to conundrums when a channel runs aground

Of unexpected life's cessation. "Something quickly must be found

To be fit into the dead air we will broadcast in a few.

Not content with being crazy, now she's kicked the bucket too.

It was just my luck she'd choose today to keep her date with doom."

With a shrug the lead producer put the issue to the room.

"Advertisers furious have threatened to debase,

For aligning them beside the charred and incandescent face

Of the Theorist ablaze, our channel, via pulling cash.

For that harpy left us naked when she turned herself to ash!

If we cannot find a substitute to keep us on the air

Then we might as well have joined her!" It was Skane who said "Beware

That in panicking we use a bland solution in this pinch.

It so happens I've a show to make the dullest viewer flinch!"

Skane proffered a dossier. "I've waited for this day

When the channel was in turmoil. Have you heard of Sally-Mae

And her tyranny of quackery? An evil empire ripe

For excoriation through the application of the type

Of bombastic revelation which the company arrayed

Here before me are adept. If I may be bold, I've made

Preparations, surely proving I've the precognition sight,

To unleash this cannonade upon the viewership tonight!

"Evidence from relatives who early were bereaved
By a diagnosis mythical, or testimony weaved
From the dying words, or living ones, upon a regimen
Mostly sugar pills and water, told through breaths of oxygen,
With establishing vignettes of solemn eyes and IV stands,
Juxtaposed with infomercials pushing Sally-Mae's own brands,
And reports of regulators, and the bribery prevailed
To obscure the recommending that this Sally-Mae be jailed.

"Paint her as a sorceress, a glamour-wielding crone,
Demagoguing to the peasants from a battlement of bone,
And the channel as a paladin alone to make a stand
'Gainst the Wizard-Empress with infected blood upon her hand!"
When the head of the producers read the dossier, his face
Showed a faint anticipation that his fast-eroding place
Was redeemable. He said "Our future may not be forlorn!
This is garbage, but we'll run it. Get the sponsors on the horn!"

Far across the city, where a castle grey and bleak
Overlooked a stretch of industry, the Gaoler gave a peek
To investors who aspired to funding every cell and wall
And recoup their offered lucre to the sound of gavel's fall.
They convened among the tower and incarceration blocks
Of the Gaoler's great creation, past a multitude of locks ,
In the warden's office, panelled walls and every fitting gilt,
In a mockery of all from which the Gaoler's worth was built.
"When Proposal 94 has fallen in the dust

Of a vigorous campaign of slander, gentlemen, we must
See the vacuum thus resulting full of legislation primed
To evolve as to our benefit, fortuitously timed
With construction of our project, so the benefit derive
From your generous investment. This Proposal 95,
Being drafted at this moment, shall precipitate a hail
Of the new-incarcerated pouring headlong into jail!"

Money being tight and every saving being made
To facilitate this gathering, the Warden there had paid
To selected inmates, trusted more than most incarcerees
To conduct themselves acceptably, the stingiest of fees
For their servitude in handing out the drinks and canapés
To the Gaoler's guests. The relevance of this, a trip betrays
To a time not very distant, just an hour or so before,
When a prisoner called Talon heard a knocking at his door.

Talon there beheld a man with canines made of gold,
And he knew it was a lawyer without having to be told.
"Sir, it is my understanding you have tireless sought a sign
Of redemption since the day the doctor didn't say 'benign',
And aware we were of how your niece's illness was described
By a nurse whose training made a parent calm and mollified.
With a sympathetic lilting in his voice he spoke about
How her time was ending long before the calendar ran out.

"Wondrous would this world appear if healing for her ills
Yet existed to be realised by joining of the wills
Of her family. But never more shall wonder be required,
For that world is real! You live in it, salvation being sired
By the genius of Sally-Mae, the patron saint of all
Who abandonment have suffered from some scalpel-wielding thrall,
Yet from ancient knowledge only can their sickness run away.
Mr Talon, let your niece survive by will of Sally-Mae!"

"Brother, I have rotted her for more than long enough,"
Countered Talon, "never to believe a syllable of stuff
You have spewing from your mouth, unless this Sally-Mae has sight
Of advantages she wants from me." The lawyer said, "You're right!
And as you have clearly prophesied, my client, with a touch
Of her noble spirit, asked a favour, though it isn't much
For a man with all the qualities that you seem to possess."
At this Talon sighed and said, "I thought so. Let me take a guess.

"Someone needs a hastening towards a frozen slab
With incision in a Y across their torso, so the lab
Can pronounce that it was murder. Invitation they have earned
To the deep eternal kingdom where the billions have burned,
Or a journey to eternal bliss before appointed time,
The injustice cruel, but you don't care, for I will do the crime
To ensure a few percent upon my niece's chance of life.
Though I hate the task, I'll do it. In this case I'll use a knife.
"Who has so offended those who pay you for your time

They despatched you to Inferno? What abominable crime
So incensed them it was worth your fee to find a miscreant
Such as I to orchestrate a swift and murderous event?
This accursed near-cadaver, though they have no knowledge how
A penumbra of oblivion approaches even now
To erase from our existence all reality they had.
For whatever sin was judged upon, I know that it was bad."

With a smile the lawyer said, "My sources indicate
You're assigned to work the meeting with investors, starting late
In the evening, and a prisoner with standing such as you
Will attend in person to the guests." And vivid Talon knew
This pronouncement made illuminate the swords suspended high
Now descending as their threads were breaking. Heaven knew just why
It was Talon at the nexus of this storm of cruel events,
But that fate had chosen Talon had lit up his every sense.

"When I was a boy," said Talon, casting back his mind
To the crime by which the latter of his life had been defined,
"I imagined how my name would leave a deep historic scar
On the world's collective memory. A general, a star,
A philanthropist, a tyrant. But I'd never reach it, since
In a cell, the showers, laundry room, some fellow pauper prince
Would impale me in the gut and end my sorry tale without
The momentous act that student bodies hence would learn about.

"Now events conspiring loop around to me in course

Of elapsing time amid my term of state-enforced remorse.

By the timing of your offer and the magnitude of stakes

It's a most exalted corpse you want delivered. If it takes

An appalling act of violence to snatch a chance at life,

I'll commit it for her sake. But though I have the perfect knife,

I require a target first. Who shall I kill so I don't sink

My stiletto blade in error?" Said the lawyer, "Who d'you think?"

At the stroke of ten the Gaoler made to justify

The investment of his guests as, like a titan from on high

Overshadowing a city he would visit with the rage

Of his godly fists of hatred, he was stood beside a stage

Where a replica in miniature of what the money spent

Would construct upon his order, down to every kerb and vent,

Stood depicting such a monument to legal suffering

The investors felt a shiver at the vision of the thing.

Labyrinth of antiseptic concrete, steel and tile,

A conveyor belt for processing a human cargo while

Through a thousand miles of corridor, a million of cells

For containing the recidivists and charging like hotels,

With as many secret corners for the extra-legal use

When instilling in the inmates mortal terror of abuse,

There were herded into galleries most every internee

To attend at bargain wages to the needs of industry!

Tiling made resistant versus acid, cold and heat

In the cubicles arranged to form a warren fit to mete

Out the punishment for which the law, too cowardly to name

The necessity of harsh correction, terrified of blame,

Has assigned to our long-suffering and loyal personnel,

With a cleanup made convenient by use in every cell

Of a subtle channel leading to a drain set in the floor,

So the fluids siphoned off can hidden to the river pour.

"Seamlessly," the Gaoler said, "the services ensue

From arrest, conviction, sentencing, appeals, we send them through

All the stages from the shedding of inertial liberty

To conversion into staring for a thousand yards, as we

Guarantee to grind them into docile subjects, otherwise

To devolve them to unthinking lumps with dust-encrusted eyes.

And an inbuilt crematorium so inconvenience

To the city is avoided when their body travels hence.

"When the city's governance accepts the public lust

For revenge, you see my preparations here regarding just

And humane elimination of a life's essential spark.

Take a look at sundry areas kept locked away and dark

With a modular design to fit the MO of the state,

Whether bullet, rope, injection, burning, crushing with a weight,

Even guillotining, firing from artillery, the boats!

Or whatever strange procedure courtly sentencing denotes.

"Here, a wing for women! And beside, facilities
For maternity, delivering the spawn of detainees
So a citizen is hatched, then through the process moving fleet
To the execution chamber where the cycle is complete!"
With polite applause the guests appraised the Gaoler's grand reveal
And the Warden then proposed a toast, calling all to heel
The attending lags to serve a glass of wine to each. As planned,
It was Talon who stepped up to push one in the Gaoler's hand.

Talon had a scar from burns inflicted when a can
Full of gasoline was hurled in culmination of a plan
To exact revenge on Talon's gang, and wayward it had healed
To provide a pocket made of flesh where Talon had concealed,
Thus invisible to warders' hands, the implement he made
From a length of broken plumbing he had haggled for in trade
For a baggie of narcotics. Not a hero's dagger set
With engravings, fine and gilded, but a slender bayonet.

"To the future," came the toast the Gaoler made, "a place
Where from cradle to the grave the wretched live but by our grace!"
As he raised the glass, the memory of Talon's niece arose
To remind him why he served a stranger's hunger to depose
From his pinnacle the Prince who clearly comprehended not
The convicted man, who grimaced as he forced apart the spot
Where his skin concealed the weapon with its sharpened iron nib.
And he stabbed the Gaoler right between the first and second rib.
Like a puppet with its strings bisected with a knife

Went collapsing down the Gaoler as the essence of his life

Came erupting from the puncture as his murderer withdrew

From his chest the shank. The Gaoler, sprawling, gasping out, fell through

The facsimile of prison, as a titan in the throes

Of a mighty downfall devastates the ancient lands where rose

Populations now sent fleeing by the giant's dying roar.

The components of his masterpiece were scattered 'cross the floor.

Talon broke the glass and, keen to finish off his prey,

He impaled the Gaoler's neck using the broken stem. When they

Could appreciate the murder they had witnessed, every guest

From the Warden's office panicking evacuated lest

They were also on a secret list and due a ghastly fate.

The alarms proclaimed impending murder thirty seconds late.

After Talon closed the Gaoler's eyes he checked the prey was dead,

And he waited for the cops to come and shoot him in the head.

Sitting with the evening glass of rosé in the heart

Of her pink embroidered décor, where she spent the hours apart

From the bustle of the city and the sugar-coated grind

Of the day-to-day deception, rested Sally-Mae, her mind

Turned from quackery. At home she had the time to contemplate

Her position with the princes, and her forging of the fate

Of the Gaoler, with her hoping that Inferno took his hide,

Which to Sally-Mae brought comfort as the one who greased the slide.

Now sufficient time had passed for media to light

On the story of the Gaoler's butchering, she thought she might

See the posse of reporters, striving, pushing through the scrum

To appoint the newly-murdered to the ranks of martyrdom.

As if never had misfortune sent in terror to a cell

An offender for a lifetime, with commission paid as well.

A triumphant sip of wine, and she then she turned on her TV

But beheld her own depiction where the Gaoler's death should be.

From her fingers fell her glass as she beheld, bemused,

Far beneath the flaking strata of foundation she had used,

Like the silt that fills a canyon to delete its faintest trace,

To fill in the creases, deadly to her brand, upon her face

The assemblage of her features, the mascara spider limbs,

And above, the acid yellow by which other colour dims

In a heap of golden wire with dedication sculpted high

To create a temple's altar made of crunchy hair and dye.

Sally-Mae was horrified to hear narration wax

On her claims of cures miraculous, the proof by standards lax,

Giving way to fury voiced by friends and family who saw

Their acquaintances and relatives walk though her clinic door

For cessation of their suffering, to live, to win, to thrive.

But in seeking this from Sally-Mae, they never left alive.

Every picture shown to illustrate a grieving friend's decree

Was of faces robbed of hope, then given hope's facsimile.

Multiple examples while the evidence accrued,

As placebos grant a temporary lifting of the mood,

And the treatment cycles, paid for, unrefundable, ensue,

With the family discouraged, lest the stress the gains undo,

From communicating with the patient. Horror Sally-Mae

Was assaulted by to see the pictures taken every day

By a snapper with a mission and a telephoto lens,

Who had captured every gruesome sight the clinic failed to cleanse.

Thunderous the waterfall of misery to show

The cadavers that remained of the beloved souls who go

Through the psuedo-medic's regimen. But worse, an inside man

Had revealed the secret recipes the clinic's lackeys ran

Through the veins and large intestines of the people in her care,

To be shown with sunken faces given in to rank despair,

And the words of employees who had been catapulted hence,

For objecting to the horror, with a toxic reference.

Sally-Mae had recourse to a battle-hardened crew

Of expensive legal troubleshooters. Furious, she drew

From between the cushions where it lay, her mobile phone to set

An avenging band of lawyers on the enemy, when yet

More appalling imagery made her rage without restraint.

"And what does exploitation of the dying buy the saint

In her cordoned-off community, her splendid palace named

The Abode of Mercy's Angels?", the narrator smugly claimed.

Fear now flooded Sally-Mae through vein and artery
When she recognised the handsome marble lions loyally
Posted guard before the tasteful beams of artificial oak
That imparted Tudor charm upon her home. And on it spoke
As the footage from a drone encircling picked out every slate
Of surrounding buildings. Any yahoo could extrapolate
The location. Sally-Mae was gripped by terminal distress
At the fact that every citizen could figure her address.

Notable the city was for great rapidity
That occurrences acquired, and in the main catastrophe,
The attention of the populace, so, even at this hour,
Being late, the grim indictment met the hunger to devour
Of the bulk of those who couldn't sleep. Among them was the lord
Of the city hospital, while checking on the coma ward.
With the sight of Sally-Mae's domain appearing on the screen
Set above the nurse's desk, the Doctor pondered on the scene.

"Interesting times I find myself alive amid,
As the Princes fall like rotten fruit for sins until now hid,
With the gale that shakes the regal bough, the rope that makes the noose,
The accumulated data we have called the Golden Goose.
On the air I taste with sureness born of intellect and wit
The annihilation pending for a craven hypocrite!
Such a pleasure it will be to witness Sally-Mae excised,
Leaving two of us, a situation I would have devised!
"That disgrace to medicine has sealed her dismal fate,

But it takes a mind of brilliance to now appreciate
How alacrity of purpose puts a scalpel in my hand
For removing a vestigial, unnecessary gland,
Like a lancet for the draining of the pus beneath the skin,
Or for cutting out a parasite intent on sucking in
The enrichment that is mine by great intelligence's right.
I've an operation planned, I cut the flesh apart tonight."

One concocted tidings for the future, while across
The departments of the city, the approaching tide was loss
Of a future. Sally-Mae had seen her phone light up as all
Her associates, on watching, vied to be the first to call
And a saviour appear by swiftly raising the alarm
And accumulate the favour, saving Sally-Mae from harm.
But as rapid as the warnings came, the best of them recede
As the city's rage was mobilised with supernature's speed.

Like the vanguard of an army slaughtered long before,
Now arisen from the battlefield still sodden with their gore
And enabled by the hatred's flame in every fleshless breast
To advance upon the traitor who, by enemy's request,
Had by sly and cunning false command condemned them to expire
And their ranks of armoured bodies made a bloody, clotted mire,
So appeared among leylandii and the replica décor
A battalion in darkness marching grim towards her door.

By a flame that leapt into a hand, she saw a face,

Not a spirit full of vengeance made reality apace,

But a citizen, unnamed among the masses of the land,

Not a blood-encrusted sabre but a petrol bomb in hand.

Then behind them, in a sequence, more were lit in orange flare

As they put the spark to Molotovs and reached the garden stair

Where the stony lions stood a useless guard. In the estate

The inhabitant was fleeing from her incandescent fate.

Not the servant's exit tucked behind a wall of flowers

Nor the sauna wherein Sally-Mae would sweat away the hours

Could afford an exit past the closing noose. She sought the name

Of a contact who could pluck her from this cauldron, when the flame

Cannonaded through the window trailing embers from its rag

To disgorge its burning paraffin across the pastel shag.

Then the fusillade of missiles shattered every outer pane

And by instinct Sally-Mae knew she would never lie again.

Lined in orange, faces every colour, age and cast,

Mutely watching as the fiery fingers tore apart the last

Of the barriers protecting Sally-Mae. No master led,

But by silent common will they had descended for her head.

They were drawn from the afflicted by the onerous belief

Their position at the corners of the spiderweb of grief

Was a paralysing sanction to their vengeance. Now they knew

With the advent of the broadcast, retribution could be due.

Through the patterned curtains, stark against a flare of red,

They espied a silhouette in frantic motion as it fled

From the living room to dining hall as panelling veneers

Caught alight. And on she sprinted through a rain of chandeliers,

Up the staircase to the bedrooms where the lavender and pink

Of upholstery were sustenance for hungry flame to drink.

As she scrambled up the attic steps she took a breath within

Of the choking smoke that billowed from the ceiling falling in.

Through the red caldera at the crown of the estate

Came the fleeing Sally-Mae, on blistered hands across the slate

And surrounded by a cloud of embers, swarming thick and bright

As a host of friendly fireflies hunting harbour to alight,

When a spark encountered wayward strands of monumental hair,

And a flash as harsh as lightning split the hot nocturnal air.

For her habit was to soak her hair, with practiced expertise,

In a plethora of products known to catch alight with ease.

Heavens torn by comet's wrath, a sable ocean rent

By a burning spear! A shattered star! A flaming missive sent

By a wrathful god! So shot a vivid bolt ablaze and pure

To the zenith of the midnight sky from Sally-Mae's coiffure.

The observers saw the gavel of their justice bearing down

Underneath a spreading incandescence such as made the frown

Of the testing of an atom bomb. And Sally-Mae was gone

When she fell into the flame to join Inferno's echelon.

Though the quack's obituary was for now unread,

Yet the Doctor with such certainty considered her as dead

He refocused on the summit. "Let us meet her in Research,"

Said the Doctor to an underling. "If hoping to besmirch

My ambition seeking knowledge, Legion's savage tongue be stayed

By the evidence of brilliance medicinal arrayed.

Now ensure that no disturbances will my attention grab!

If an urgent case presents itself, I'll see it on the slab."

Underneath the wards and waiting-rooms, well out of mind,

Past the signage warning biohazards waited just behind,

Was a wing of white dissection-rooms with drainage in the floors

And incinerators leading off refrigerated stores.

At the centre, a theatre with the seating full around

Where anatomists could lecture on the wonders to be found

In cadavers pared apart as neat as petals from a bloom.

It was here the Doctor waited, silent, thinking in the gloom.

Legion kept him waiting. When she walked in through the door

Of the hospital she left her lackeys on the upper floor,

For the Princes, when a pair of them had matters to debate

Would permit no hangers-on around to dare participate.

So alone it was she passed the shelves of jars of pickled brains,

Through the stink of disinfectant over curdling remains.

When she entered the anatomy theatre without fear,

There the Doctor offered, "Glad that you could make it, sister dear."

"If you were my brother, Doctor, I would spit upon

The pollution of my bloodline," Legion countered. "I have gone

All my lifetime without counting such as you as family,

And I have no more intention of beginning now than we

Have of casting off the wealth for which our hands alone have worked."

"It's so funny you should mention that," the Doctor said, and smirked.

"I can make a guess why into this asylum I was led,"

She continued. "I can't help but notice most of us are dead.

"Vermin gutted, all the matters on the Prophet's mind

Spread across the wall. The Theorist was cancelled and unkind

It may be to say but well-deserved. The Gaoler with a shank

Sent careening off the mortal coil. The citizens to thank

For dear Sally-Mae's annihilation. Now I've got them all,"

Said the Doctor, "As you rightly say, we have to make the call."

"Do we split the Golden Goose between us, make content with half,

Or shall violence ensue?" said Legion with a bitter laugh.

"Compromise, a filthy word, yet one I stoop to use,"

She said. "War's alternative it is. I have no wish to lose

So immense an empire fighting for the Golden Goose entire,

And especially when you're across the battlefield. Retire

From the tedium of Princes pushing pieces as they play,

And instead become the sovereigns of kingdoms far away

From each other. When we make the Golden Goose regurgitate

Its torrential tide of riches, let survivors separate."

"Keep us well apart, like fighting dogs in heat for now?"
Mused the Doctor with a pause and thoughtful furrow of the brow.
"I'd say let us lay foundations for avoidance of a tiff,
And for thrashing out a treaty for its observation, if
My associates above had done their job for once and found
The revolver loaded, ready, in the holster strapped around
Your delightful torso. Knowing human bodies as I do,
Its inelegant dimensions made it obvious on you."

At the Doctor's accusations Legion tried to draw
From its sheath the gun she carried, but a gnarled and useless claw
She perceived where there had been her fingers closed upon the grip,
But unable now to function, hanging feeble at her hip.
Her pronunciation straining from her locking jaw she spat,
"What atrocity besets me, you cadaver-carving rat?
I had hoped to shoot you, by our standards frank diplomacy,
Yet your wicked hand inflicts some toxic malady on me!"

Minutes passed in which the Doctor pointedly admired,
Like a master sculptor carving from the marble block, inspired
To evoke the human form with a specific reference
To expressions of disdainful scorn and terror, both intense,
The paralysis-affected shape of Legion, held in place,
Quite immobile save an eyelid twitch and spasm of the face.
"There's no doubt," opined the Doctor, "that your torpitude and pain
Make you crave an understanding. Lucky you, I can explain.
"Many my ambitions were, but one above them fired

My imagination well beyond my studies. I desired
A concoction rapid-acting and infallible to send
All the function of the human nervous system round the bend
Save the vitals, respiration and the beating of the heart,
The digestive system, organs of the senses and the part
Of the brain that sifts the information flood the senses bring
And provides an understanding of the body's suffering.

"Thus I join the firmament of Curie, Boyle and Planck,
And recalibrate the standard model! Future minds will thank
The crusading knight of knowledge stood before you for the gift
I bestow upon the world through endless battling to lift
The restrictions of the timid and the fawning from the task
Of the scientific method. Even now you surely ask,
Or you would if you could vocalise, by what means can I speak
When I breathe the same concoction that has left you gravely weak?"

Silence with a garnish of intense and hateful glare
Was the answer Legion gave. The Doctor lectured, "while the air
Is suffused with paralytic agent, just before the time
Of your entrance to the hospital, I thought it wise to prime
My anatomy by hypodermic needle to the vein
With an antidote to counter diminution of the brain.
Thus retaining all my faculties while rendering you forlorn,
Though I fear the side effects on my intestines in the morn.

"Cunning for one proud of how her hands abhor the scent

Of the blood shed by her enemies, to come here with intent

Of eliminating me in person! Surely that's the last

Course of action I'd anticipate. Yet intellect of vast

And superior potential you encountered. Never fear!

I'm no monster. My hands also shall be clean of blood, my dear."

So the Doctor wheeled a gurney to the chamber's central stage

And he wheeled the stricken Legion from the room, and off the page.

Deeper than the Doctor's sanctum, ever more malign

Than the morgues and vivisection rooms, a warren clandestine

Where experimental treatments on behalf of clientele

Were conducted far from oversight. A plain and sterile cell

Was repeated down the corridors. The staining on the walls

Told a story the authorities would learn of not at all.

In the oubliette of aeons, at the very lowest pit,

Were the batteries of boxes where a human frame could fit.

Many was the pharmacist whose newest remedy

Was untried upon a human, but a quick fatality

Was a likelihood, so lawful testing could not be approved.

For a payout huge and undeclared, the Doctor could be moved

To acquire a coma patient whose demise could be explained

As a consequence of nature's malice. Suitably contained

In a crate beneath the hospital, they gave a means to peek

At the horrors on the body the medicament could wreak.

One among the guinea-pigs was Legion, paralysed

For the time it took to prep her body, locking her inside
With a feeding tube and drip to help ensure her tenancy
Was the natural extension of her life expectancy,
And a catheter inserted so her waste would not collect,
Then a freezing automatic spray to clean and disinfect.
With extremities restrained so thrashing limbs could never break,
She was just like all the others, only Legion was awake.

Sole among the Princes, lone survivor of the Blitz,
That endowed the city streets with broken corpses, by the glitz
And accumulated power made to rule their demimonde
Now reduced to meat and bloody bone, in Legion's case beyond
Comprehension of the city. Now the Doctor walked alone
Through the hospital's environs knowing no-one could dethrone
The possessor of the Golden Goose, inviolate, complete,
And he mused upon a future with such luxury replete.

Deftly turned the Doctor's mind to saturating light
That suffused a lifetime funded by the proceeds of the might
Now afforded to the sole surviving Prince. A nurse's screen
Drawn between the fate of Legion and the bedlam sunk between
The forgotten comas' labyrinth and hospital. His gait
Was a strutting wholly heedless of the eminence of hate
Fairly pulsing past the corner. With his senses uninvolved
He avoided comprehending how his destiny resolved.

Twining skeins of arbitrary fate, ever in flux,

Forming warp and weft unceasing with the Doctor at the crux,

In a pattern of the red of blood and white of broken bone,

But invisible to kismet's prey, who, deafened to the drone

Of the end descending, to the stench of his own rotting form

Made oblivious, saw nothing there around him but the norm!

So without a fear the Doctor strode with joy in every pace,

Round a corner, to be halted by the sight of Vermin's face.

Science lost its primacy, the Doctor's wisdom failed

To account for how the Prince pariah's butchered soul had sailed

From beyond the veil of death that hangs opaque across the gate

Of the kingdom of the dead. Yet Vermin stood to desecrate

The inviolate commandments of a mortal pagandom,

In appropriate a manner for the Prince of Odium.

In a bloody gown was Vermin wrapped, with ties along the back

Such as patients there were given, and his eyes were ringed in black.

Stupid with alarm, the Doctor uttered, "you were dead!"

Then the Prince of Rats, a hand upon the Doctor's shoulder, said,

"Did you truly think a fountainhead of malice such as I,

Such a welling-up of loathing, such embodied hate, could die?

Were I buried in the grave, my hate would leach into the ground

And the very dirt and lichen wrap my skeleton around

With the headstone held upon my back to crush what I despise,

And the sockets of my eyes a nest of maggots, I arise!

"Folly to believe such an existence could have been,

By an exorcism powered by a dagger in the spleen,

For eternity truncated, let alone when by the force

Of the pasty hand of Gideon directed! Yes, of course,

I've a mutilation grave enough to earn a man a tag,

And I'll spend my life remaining defecating in a bag,

But then Doctor, surely we of all the people know about

All the body parts a man can lose and yet survive without!

"Revelled I in memories to hear the nurses scream

As I woke up during surgery from sleep without a dream

They mistook for death's oblivion. Already they had called

For an orderly to cart away my corpse when I, appalled

By the sheer audacity it took to ever think me fit

For a sacrifice, sat up and felt the stitches in the slit

Down my belly tear, the pain of sundered guts a signal clear

That alive I was, and trailing my intestines, made it here.

"Since my forced and temporary failure to exist,

Near a night has passed, so tell me, was there anything I missed?"

Here the Doctor let a knowing smile appear across his face

And said "Son, events have overtaken you at quite a pace!

Of the Princes none but you and I survive, yet I proclaim

That our mourning shall be eased by what the fates have seen remain

From the riches of our brethren. Let us dry our bitter tears

On the wads of cash collected from the coffers of our peers.

"Think on all the luxuries denied to you as long

As the Princes pulled the strings. I never thought you could belong,

I'll admit. But now the rest are gone I'll grant the honours due

For the grim and filthy labours we would delegate to you."

In the wake of such an offer, Vermin played at giving thought

To division of the city's bounty. Then he said, "I ought

To correct you on an error making all you say a sham.

For about the Golden Goose, I really couldn't give a damn.

"I had put the map together long before I died

Of how Gideon congealed his lump of filthy cash. If I'd

Had the slightest of intentions to partake of all he took,

Then I would have flayed his bank accounts and watched the donnybrook

As the accusations fell upon the Prophet's fellow scum.

The desire for wealth and luxury, my lusts have overcome.

I've a thirst that only flesh and horror have the force to slake.

What I want you cannot give me. What I want, I have to take."

"Name it and I'll make it happen," said the Doctor, yet,

The inflection in his fearful voice against his words was set

As his eyes flicked down the corridor in hope against despair

He would find security with weapons drawn approaching there.

But he'd sent them all away to open Legion's final door.

That's when Vermin held an ID up, the kind the mortals wore

With employment at the hospital. He said, "this bit of gear

Was observed in my possessions when they brought my carcass here.

"Pity he who sent me after Gideon, intent

On my sacrifice ensuing! For on guessing how he meant

To entice me through the promise of the Prophet's branded wench

Into suffering his sacrificial vengeance, with a wrench

Of my wrist in application of a youth of larceny,

I abstracted from his pocket proof of who the fool could be.

No surprise above the surname 'Skane', the hospital was named.

How convenient to wake so close to he who should be blamed!"

"Never was this person, Skane, brought into my employ!

For your vengeance, seek another," said the Doctor without joy

In demanding from the empty wards a baton-wielding aide.

Still advancing, Vermin sneered "an honour grand and yet unmade

I bestow on you! For witness how I flout a single time

The belief that hope and honesty are met by not a crime

In severity or punishment. Against the rule I fly,

For the truth is, I've a scalpel, and my hope is you will die."

Atlas, cervical, thoracic, lumbar vertebrae,

Intercostal muscles, pulsing mass of lungs, compelled to lay

Raw and open to the disinfected air, the legacy

Of the Doctor's nerve collapsing as he turned around to flee.

With the scalpel gleaming, Vermin leapt and plunged the weapon's tip

In the Doctor's shoulder, carving through from scapula to hip.

As his face the floor impacted hard, the Doctor's sense of pain

Was alerted to the scalpel punching through his flesh again.

All the strength in Vermin's torn and ravaged body poured
In a torrent into mutilation, waxing anger stored
At a world appalled to witness him and all but him bestowed,
At the knowledge deeply hidden his frustrated fury flowed
From the wrongs he nurtured constant yet would rather die again
Than acknowledge how a flock of evils roosted in his brain.
All the helpless fury, buried shame, descended hot and raw
To impel the scalpel through the Doctor, scraping on the floor.

Somewhere in the welling-up of blood, the Doctor's breath
Was arrested in his throat and Vermin, drinking of the death
Like a parasite, its sustenance from suckling at the fount
Of a violent and recent slaying, Vermin took account
Of the bedlam he had made of muscle, bone and skin. His thirst
Thusly sated by the execution, stood up, looking first
For a weapon more substantial than the scalpel he had bent
On the Doctor's fragile skeleton, he pondered his intent.

"Let the Golden Goose fall prey to withering neglect,
For the money is of no use to me. Much finer to elect
The indulgence of the hunger ever clawing at my head
For humiliation, power, pretty eyes reflecting dread!
In the bedlam of the Prince's absence, surfeit let erupt
Of protection now rescinded from authorities corrupt
That a regiment of women once relied upon. No more
Will a promise made for payment keep the hunter from their door!
"Paint upon this foetid world a bloody rictus grin

And upon the earth a harvest sow of misery and sin,

So a caul of suffering erupts and oozes from the crack

Of the filthy streets, a suppurating, gelid mass to wrack

This whole city with a pain to strike the people with a pox,

With paralysis that life, vitality and passion mocks,

So from broken bodies grows a crop of fleshly scraps of hell,

And I gambol through the fields of gore, my hunger sated well!

"Could a lack of blood have put that wonderland of hate

In my head, and ravaged innards helped inspire me to create

An insane amalgamation of my crimson-tinted dreams?

Does it matter? While my body lasts I'm chasing down the means

To evoke it as reality and walk it live or dead."

As he muttered this soliloquy, the wounded Vermin bled

Out a ragged scarlet river, every footstep red and bright,

Through the waiting room and entrance doors, and out into the night.

On a square of tarmac by the hospital façade

Where the ambulances parked, a tempting sight to disregard,

Was a figure in a suit possessing nothing much distinct,

Yet demanding Vermin's eye. A spark of recognition linked

To decisions made to murder, codified and set aside

For the future. Vermin called out, "You who stands there! Crucified

Would I be had I not every face in memory installed

That I'd sworn one day to kill. And thus your face I have recalled.

"You were Skane the waiter who the Prophet's whore revealed

And attained for me the fate evisceration nearly sealed,

But your name's association with this place led me to saw

Through the one intact umbilical to how it was before.

Now a new and wondrous world awaits my vital appetite!

I have you to thank!" But Vermin's eyes, adjusting to the night,

Could perceive the kill, which first appeared the simplest he had known,

Would be hindered by the novel fact that Skane was not alone.

Turbulent the night a storm of death had thrown about

With a thrill upon the wind that drew the population out

In anticipation more would fall, the televised demise

With an encore illustrated by the way the embers rise

From the conflagrated mansion. On the corners, porches, streets,

There were citizens awaiting news of who next fate deletes.

So when Skane addressed the city in response to Vermin's sneer,

There were plenty gathered thereabouts, and primed for news to hear.

Bloody-tinged upheaval! Anarchistic end of days!

So the cityscape was shifting in abrupt and brutal ways,

And the people, long exhausted by the Princes' lustful scorn,

Were content to let the current drag them through to savage dawn.

"Hear me sisters, daughters, mothers, wives, and all who hold them dear,"

Came the call from Skane, "If not yourselves, then someone very near,

Is acquainted with the face of that bedraggled streak of skin

As it leered among the shadows with its broken yellow grin!

"Taste the fear, its oily reek suffusing through the air,

At its source the spectre in the bloody gown, awaiting there

The decision of the people on his clandestine career

Of indulging cruder instinct with a condiment of fear,

An induction into victimhood decided by a lack

Of forewarning, strength or circumstance required to fight him back!

Let a novelty commence as we an education give

On the nature of a target having ample means to live!"

"Better men, in droves, I faced, and bleeding left them all!

So come on you slags, if all at once, then all at once you'll fall!"

But as Vermin spat defiance, they surrounded him as one

In a cordon drawing closer. With a start, as if to run,

He beheld the fists and faces of a living barricade,

With his scalpel gripped as tightly as the pin on a grenade.

If an apprehension sparked to see the starlight on the steel,

They betrayed it not, for closely-packed, they had no room to feel.

Vermin sought an exit as they closed with every pace

And the scalpel barely flickered when the pavement hit his face.

The accumulated bodies served to pin him underneath.

With their fists and feet they started, but they finished with their teeth.

And as many were the souls impelling force through skin and bone,

There were none of them could say they were a murderer alone,

Thus a truth revealed far deeper was than murder as an art,

As by limb by sinew, muscle, tendon, Vermin came apart.

Under the assault of knuckle, forehead, tooth and shoe,

His resolve began to falter as his elbow tore in two.

When his shoulder left the socket, Vermin's overwrought disease

Of bravado ebbed. Defiance turned to fury, then to pleas,

Then to begging for another minute drawing ragged breath,

With a desperation sharpened by the rasping sound of death

That was broken bone on concrete and of leather into skin,

And the splintering of many ribs amid their caving in.

Still on Vermin's lips the fevered, babbling release

Of apology, contrition, begging, bargaining to cease

The dividing and deforming of the matter of his clay

Into which a life was breathed at birth, now ebbing swift away.

His penultimate pronouncement lost in gargled spurts of gore

All upwelling from his abdomen as flesh and organ tore,

With the final sound a rising scream of high and piercing tone

Then a silence only broken by the sullen crunch of bone.

Somewhere in the heaving bedlam, Vermin sputtered out,

And the vital sparked was earthed. Unburdened now by any doubt

The offending soul might still be resident, their aim achieved,

His assailants, by the vicious flurry now exhausted, grieved

For the hours that went in solitude that others should have shared,

Or the brutal, helpless dreams that formed the wake of he who stared

From the ground, the face the only clue a human once retained

The possession of the butcher's worth of offal that remained.

Blooming in a flower, crimson-petalled, symmetry

Now unravelled as if battered in a storm incessantly,

With a spinal column stamen, lung and stomach stigma rent

By ungentle ministrations of the crowd, their fervour spent,

As they turned their back as one against the once-was-human thing,

With agreements made in silence that they never saw a thing,

They were never here, and if they were, he couldn't have survived,

For he met his fate beforehand and was dead when they arrived.

Face to face, brutality, no screen or distance, had

Until now to Skane been absent. But the sight of wilting, sad

And repulsive parts of Vermin told a story of the dead

He could not ignore, no matter how by justice he was led.

By his hand, if at a distance, he had killed and killed again,

In the knowledge every Prince would fall as surely as the rain.

So, confronted by the stench of voided bowels and guts arrayed,

The acceptance it was over on his back unyielding weighed.

Murky dawn's attempt to climb the skyline had begun

So the early smog was rosy with the efforts of the sun,

As scintillas played across the gleaming surface of the gore

And its face was barely darkened by the rising smoke that bore

The component parts of Sally-Mae to mingle as it waned

With the echoes of the Theorist's demise, and what remained

Of the night's appalling news within the electronic waves

Now diminishing, the city turning calmer than its graves.

iolence I railed against, but violence I dealt,"
Pondered Skane to no one listening. "But contrary, I felt
That inaction was complicity when blatant is the ill,
Even wickedness in error this is justified. But still…"
No assurance from the Dawn there came and Skane had always known
The conundrum of his deeds and consequence were his alone.
"Maybe I just wrote a fairy tale where everybody died,"
He considered to himself. "But what the hell, at least I tried."

If there was a goddess, she would sing about the chill
Of a morning when the silence came, avenging, down to fill
Where the din of brute aggression was deleted in a rain
Of exsanguination running in the gutters. Now the bane
Of the city was no longer seven parasites enthroned,
But the future undetermined. Not by violence atoned
Of their evils, now the tyrants' hands were bleeding torn away,
So the city heard a dreadful freedom breaking with the day.